MOONGAME

A MOONBEAR *Book*

■ FRANK ASCH ■

ALADDIN

NEW YORK   LONDON   TORONTO   SYDNEY   NEW DELHI

ALADDIN

An imprint of Simon & Schuster Children's Publishing Division

1230 Avenue of the Americas, New York, NY 10020

This Aladdin edition March 2014

For information about special discounts for bulk purchases, please contact

Simon & Schuster Special Sales at 1-866-506-1949 or business@simonandschuster.com.

The Simon & Schuster Speakers Bureau can bring authors to your live event.

For more information or to book an event contact the Simon & Schuster Speakers Bureau

at 1-866-248-3049 or visit our website at www.simonspeakers.com.

Designed by Karina Granda

The text of this book was set in Olympian LT Std.

Manufactured in China 1213 SCP

10 9 8 7 6 5 4 3 2 1

The Library of Congress has cataloged a previous edition as follows:

Asch, Frank. Moongame

Summary: During a game of hide and seek, Moon hides behind a cloud,

leaving his friend Bear very worried.

[1. Hide-and-seek—Fiction. 2. Animals—Fiction. 3. Moon—Fiction.] I. Title.

PZ7.A778Mpf   1988   [E]   88-6572

ISBN 978-1-4424-9407-7 (hc)

ISBN 978-1-4424-9406-0 (pbk)

ISBN 978-1-4424-9408-4 (eBook)

To Devin, Amanda, Rachel, Megan, Sam, Caleb,
Jeremy, Lindsey, Chris, Daniel, and Luke

One day Little Bird showed Bear a new game: hide-and-seek. First he told Bear to hide and counted to ten: 1, 2, 3, 4, 5, 6, 7, 8, 9, 10.

Then he went looking for Bear.

"I found you!" chirped Little Bird when he found Bear hiding behind some bushes. "Now it's your turn to find me!"

All day long, until the sun went down, Bear and Little Bird played their new game.

That night when Bear was all alone, he looked up in the sky and said to the moon, "Let's play hide-and-seek! First I'll hide and you'll find me."

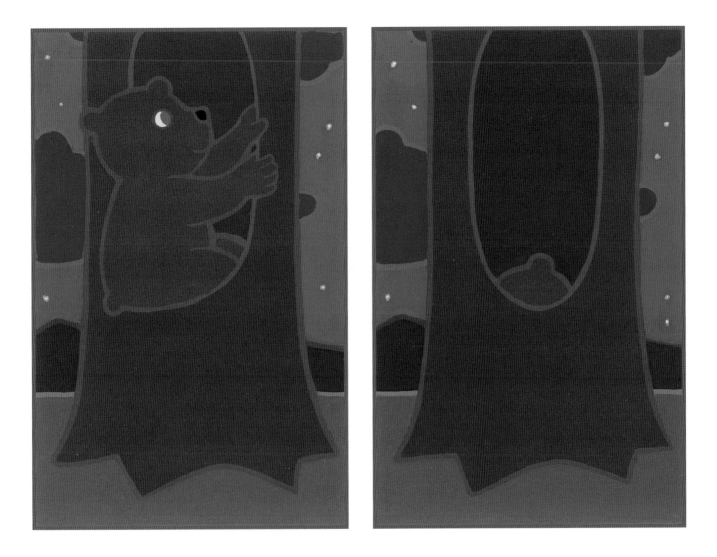

Then Bear ran as fast as he could until he came to an old hollow tree.

Climbing inside, he ducked down so the moon couldn't see him.

Bear waited for a while, then he poked his head up. When he did, the moon was right there looking down at him.

"Okay," said Bear, "you found me. Now it's your turn to hide."

Closing his eyes, Bear began to count just as Little Bird had shown him.

At that moment a gentle breeze

slowly hid the moon behind a big cloud.

When Bear finished counting, he set out to find the moon.
First he thought he found the moon hiding behind some
rocks.

Then he thought he found the moon hiding in someone's house.

When Bear thought he found the moon hiding in a tree, he shook the tree and cried, "I found you, Moon!"

But Bear was mistaken.

All he found was a big balloon.

Then Little Bird came by to visit.

"Will you help me find the moon?" asked Bear.

"Sure, I'll help," chirped Little Bird.

Bear and Little Bird looked and looked, but they couldn't find the moon.

So they went to the forest to ask for help.

"I think the moon is lost," explained Bear. "Can you help me find him?"

"Don't worry, we'll help you," replied the animals in the forest.

Together they searched and searched.

But they couldn't find the moon.

At last Bear sat down and sighed. "The moon is lost and it's all my fault!"

Then Bear got an idea.

He jumped up and cried, "Okay, Moon, I give up. You win!"

Just then the breeze began to blow again,

and the moon came out of its hiding place.

"Look," chirped Little Bird. "The moon wasn't lost. He was just hiding behind that big cloud."

Bear was so happy he danced and danced.

Then everyone played hide-and-seek.